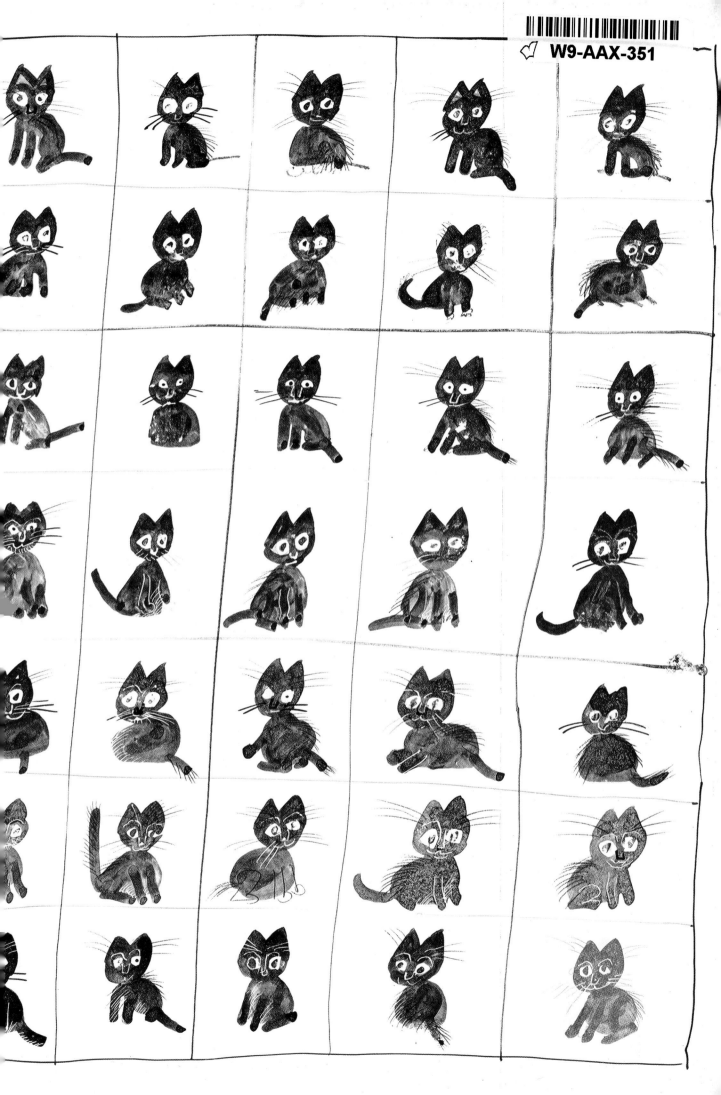

Kalikah

VIKING
Published by the Penguin Group
Viking Penguin, a division of Penguin Books USA Inc.,
375 Hudson Street, New York, New York 10014, U.S.A.
Penguin Books Ltd, 27 Wrights Lane, London W8 5TZ, England
Penguin Books Australia Ltd, Ringwood, Victoria, Australia
Penguin Books Canada Ltd, 2801 John Street, Markham, Ontario, Canada L3R 1B4
Penguin Books (N.Z.) Ltd, 182–190 Wairau Road, Auckland 10, New Zealand

Penguin Books Ltd, Registered Offices: Harmondsworth, Middlesex, England

First published in Switzerland by bohem press, 1989
First American edition published in 1991
1   3   5   7   9   10   8   6   4   2
Copyright © bohem press, 1989
All rights reserved

ISBN 0-670-83707-5
Library of Congress card catalog number: 90-70731

Printed in Italy
Set in Aster

Rosie
the Cool Cat

by Piotr Wilkon
illustrated by Jozef Wilkon

Viking

In a beautiful house, on the top of Black Hill, lived Casper and Carolina Cat. In every room, they had pictures of their parents, grandparents, and great-grandparents. Everyone in the family was famous for their beautiful jet-black fur.

Casper and Carolina were looking forward to having kittens.

Finally, the big day came. When Casper saw his four jet-black kittens, he shouted, "This is the most wonderful day of my life!"

"I am not sure about that," said Carolina. "There is still one more kitten."

Amazed, Casper turned around and saw a little
kitten who looked exactly like her sisters and
brothers—except that her fur was completely
orange!

"This is terrible!" said Casper. "We've never had an orange cat in our family. What will the neighbors say?" But all Casper's sobbing and crying did not help.

Rosie paid no attention. She did just what she liked to do, and she did everything differently from her sisters and brothers.

Each day, the kittens would take a walk with their mother, and Rosie always trailed behind. All the cats in the neighborhood would watch. "There goes crazy Rosie," they whispered.

Rosie became more and more difficult. She would not drink milk. She only wanted tea.

Instead of catching mice with her brothers and sisters, Rosie played and danced with them. The neighborhood cats were so angry at Rosie that they would no longer come to Casper and Carolina's house. Casper's beautiful black fur began to turn gray.

Then Rosie decided not to sleep in the basket with her sisters and brothers. Instead, she slept outside with Punk the dog.

This was too much for Rosie's family. A friendship between a dog and a cat was not allowed.

The next day, Carolina said to her daughter: "How dare you be friends with a dog?"

"Mother," said Rosie, "I want to move away. I don't fit in here."
"But I love you!" said her mother. "Stay with us and learn to behave like a proper cat."

"I must go away," answered Rosie.

Rosie moved out and things were quiet on Black
Hill. Friends came to visit again. Casper no longer
got gray hairs and the ones he had he carefully dyed
black. But Carolina was sad, for they had heard
nothing from Rosie. Once, Uncle Carl heard that
Rosie had made some bad friends.
She had been seen hanging out with red and even
piebald cats. "It's all the fault of that horrible Punk!"
Carolina said.

Rosie had been away from home a long time. Her sisters and brothers were grown up and had their own families. One Sunday, Casper and Carolina were watching TV. Suddenly they saw Rosie on the screen! She was the star of a rock group, and her fans—cats of every color—were cheering and screaming. "Why, that's our Rosie!" Carolina cried out. "She's famous!"

"I think I'm getting some more gray hairs," replied Casper. Still, he watched the show till it was over.

A few days later, somebody knocked at the door. It was Rosie. "May I come in?" she asked. "I'd like you to meet my kittens. I wanted to come sooner, but I was busy recording my albums, and with all the performing…" Little orange balls of fur followed Rosie, and at the very end a black kitten wandered in. "Why, this one is the spitting image of me!" cried Casper. "Yes, and I named him after you, Dad," said Rosie.

"I don't know what's to become of him, though. Little Caz does everything differently from his sisters and brothers."

Carolina was very happy to see Rosie and all her kittens, and Casper had a change of heart.
Now, he only thinks about his grandchildren. They live with him sometimes, since Rosie is often on tour.

Black Hill is always full of guests now. Who wouldn't want to visit the family of such a famous rock star?